SHAD[illegible] OF A DREAMING MIND

Shanaya Alana Carena

SHADOWS OF A DREAMING MIND

GRIFFIN
publication

GRIFFIN PUBLICATION

Registration No: UDYAM-UP-56-0004439
Yashoda Kunj, Mawana Road, Meerut, 205001
First Published by GRIFFIN publication 2024

ISBN: 978-93-91813-94-9

FROM THE AUTHOR'S DESK

Dear readers

For the past few weeks, I have let my imagination run wild, diving into a fantasy world brimming with dragons, mythical creatures, and adventures beyond the ordinary. "Shadows of a Dreaming Mind" is the culmination of my dreams, ideas, and the boundless worlds I have created in my mind.

I am immensely grateful to my mom Indira Carena whose constant motivation pushed me to complete this book. Her unwavering support kept me focused and determined, even when I felt like giving up. She was my biggest cheerleader, ensuring I finished every last line of this story.

I also thank my dad, Marc Carena, for his invaluable support and for taking the time to proofread my work. His guidance and feedback have been crucial in shaping this book. And of course, a special mention goes to my elder brother, Armando, who has been my active listener to all my imaginations and is eagerly waiting to help bring this story to life through an audiobook with his amazing dramatic voice.

I dedicate this book to my grandparents, Carlo and Silviya Carena, and Shanti Devi and Ganga Sarup Vashishta, whose stories and traditions have left an indelible mark on my creative path and whose DNA I carry.

This journey of writing has been a joyous one, deeply inspired by my 3rd and 4th grade teacher, Mrs. Juliet Kantazi. She was incredibly supportive and kind to everyone she met, and her creative teaching methods, including an interesting book she used for lessons, ignited my love for storytelling. It was in her class that I discovered the magic of writing and began to explore my imagination freely. My heartfelt thanks to Mrs Suzanne Bhargava who added so much to the motivation and encouragement in my creative journey.

Thank you all for joining me on this adventure. I hope you enjoy reading "Shadows of a Dreaming Mind" as much as I enjoyed creating it.

Happy Reading

Shanaya

Contents

PROLOGUE

I live in my dreams

Only to doubt if they are real…

I live with my questions

Only to doubt if at all they have answers…

-Shanaya

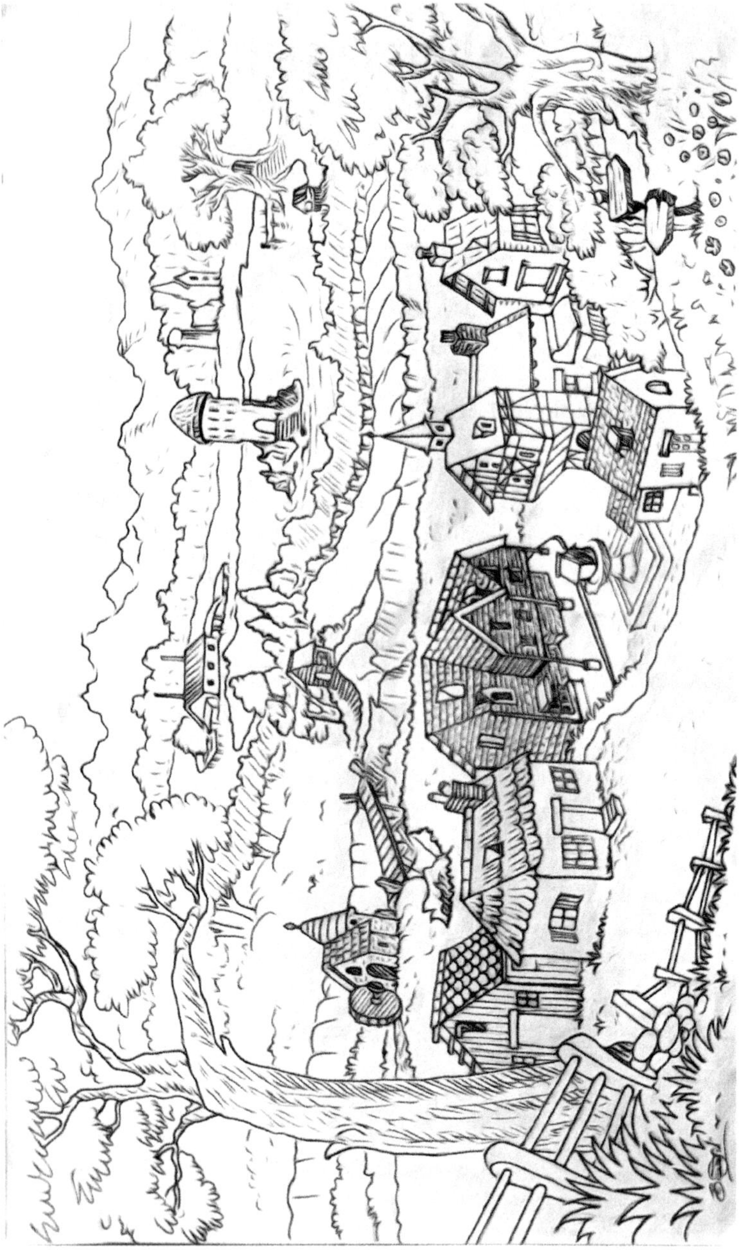

CHAPTER 1

THE NEW ENEMIES!

My name is Dondan, and I live in a small but amazing town called Eveande Carlin. Eldermere lay nestled in a serene valley, surrounded by rolling hills and dense woodlands. As dawn broke, a thick blanket of fog settled over the cobblestone streets, lending an air of mystery and tranquility to the old town.

The town's architecture was a testament to centuries gone by, with charming cottages and half-timbered houses lining the narrow, winding lanes. Each building was unique, yet they all shared a common thread of age and history, with ivy creeping up stone walls and wooden shutters that creaked in the breeze. The roofs were adorned with moss, and the chimneys, now dormant, stood like silent

sentinels against the misty sky. Tall and majestic trees bordered the town, their leaves rustling softly in the near-silence. The fog clung to their trunks and branches, casting eerie shadows and transforming the landscape into a scene from a fairy tale.

Our world is a fantasy, filled with magic and wonder, and my best friend Kaller and I have a knack for finding adventures. Kaller has blond hair, blue eyes, and thin lips. We go everywhere together. Today, we're off to the kingdom of Frzhodon to explore the Canton of Luck.

The sun was just beginning to rise, casting a golden glow over the rooftops of Eveande Carlin. I could hear the chirping of birds and the distant sounds of our town waking up. Kaller arrived at my house, his eyes sparkling with excitement.

"Ready, Dondan?" Kaller asked, his voice filled with anticipation.

"Absolutely! Let's go before it gets too crowded," I replied, slinging my satchel over my shoulder.

We waved goodbye to our parents and set off down the cobblestone streets, the morning air crisp and refreshing. As we walked, we talked about all the amazing things we might find in the Canton of Luck.

The journey to Frzhodon was filled with laughter and excitement. The landscape changed from rolling hills to dense forests, and finally to the majestic gates of the kingdom. The Canton of Luck was bustling with people, all eager to try their fortune.

"Wow, look at that, Dondan!" Kaller pointed at a massive wheel of fortune in the center of the square.

But before we could get closer, a shadow fell over us. A man, tall and menacing, grabbed us

by the collars. His eyes were cold, and his grip was like iron.

"Where do you think you're going, kids?" he sneered.

Kaller and I exchanged frightened glances. My heart was pounding in my chest. Who was this man, and what did he want with us? Just as panic started to set in, a city guard appeared and seized the man, dragging him away.

"You boys alright?" the guard asked, his face stern but kind.

"Y-yes, sir. Thank you," I stammered.

The guard nodded. "Be careful. That man is a wanted criminal. You're lucky I got here in time."

Shaken but determined not to let the incident ruin our day, Kaller and I continued exploring the Canton. After a while, we decided to venture into the nearby woods. The trees were

tall and ancient, their leaves whispering secrets to those who dared to listen.

"Let's see what's over there," Kaller suggested, pointing to a dark cave hidden behind a thicket.

We squeezed through the bushes and found ourselves in a cavernous space. The air was thick with the smell of moss and damp earth.

"This place is cool," I said, my voice echoing off the walls.

But then Kaller froze, his eyes wide with horror. "Dondan, look!"

Underneath the leaves, we saw the unmistakable legs of five or six dragons. Before we could react, Kaller accidentally stepped on a tail hidden under a pile of moss.

The dragons roared in unison, their eyes snapping open. Panic surged through me as we bolted for the entrance. Kaller kept

shouting, "SORRY!" while we ran, our breaths coming in ragged gasps.

The ground shook as the dragons pursued us. We sprinted through the forest, our feet barely touching the ground. Just when I thought we were done, we spotted an opening between two massive trees. We dove through it, barely making it to safety.

The dragons couldn't fit through the narrow gap. Their frustrated roars faded into the distance as we collapsed on the ground, panting and trembling.

When we finally caught our breath, we looked at each other and burst out laughing, the adrenaline making everything seem surreal.

"Let's not tell anyone about the dragons," Kaller said, still chuckling. "They'll think we're crazy."

Shamaya

I nodded in agreement. "Yeah, who just wanders into a dragon's den anyway? Well, apparently we do!"

As we made our way back to the Canton of Luck, the sun was setting, casting a warm, golden glow over the kingdom. Despite the scare, we felt a sense of accomplishment. We had faced danger and come out the other side, our friendship stronger than ever.

That evening, as we sat by the fountain in the town square, Kaller turned to me with a serious expression.

"Dondan, promise me we'll always stick together, no matter what adventures we find."

I smiled and nodded. "I promise, Kaller. No matter what."

And with that, we watched the stars begin to twinkle in the sky, dreaming of the adventures that awaited us in our magical world.

CHAPTER 2

HOW DID WE GET THERE EXACTLY?

Kaller and I made a silent pact not to speak of our harrowing encounter with the dragons. Instead, we decided to clear our minds with a walk in the familiar forest surrounding Eveande Carlin. The forest, with its towering trees and the faint scent of pine in the air, had always been our sanctuary. Little did we know, this walk would lead us into another adventure.

The sun was beginning to set, casting long shadows on the forest floor. As we walked, the sounds of chirping birds and rustling leaves created a soothing symphony. Suddenly, a flicker of light caught our attention.

“Did you see that, Kaller?” I asked, pointing towards the light.

Kaller nodded, his blue eyes wide with curiosity. "Let's check it out."

We followed the light, which seemed to beckon us deeper into the forest. It moved swiftly, darting behind trees and through bushes. We hurried after it, our hearts pounding with excitement and a touch of fear. Just as we thought we had it cornered, the light vanished into thin air.

"What just happened?" Kaller asked, bewildered.

"I don't know," I replied, looking around. "But this place... it doesn't look familiar."

We were lost. The once comforting forest now felt eerie and unwelcoming. The sky had darkened, and a thick fog rolled in, making it hard to see even a few feet ahead. Panic started to set in.

"I can't see my town," I exclaimed, my voice trembling.

"Me neither," Kaller said, equally frightened. "What are we going to do?"

The forest, which usually teemed with life, was now silent and foreboding. Every rustle of leaves or snap of a twig made us jump. In a world where anything was possible, our imaginations ran wild. Could it be a skinwalker? A monster? Or even a ghost?

We huddled close together, shivering in our boots. Suddenly, a figure emerged from the shadows. It was unlike anything we had ever seen before. A man, but made entirely of leaves and wood, stepped forward. He had glasses perched on his leafy nose and spoke with a distinctly British accent.

"Ho hello! Are you visitors? Or inspectors?" the leaf man asked with uncertainty.

"Um, no sir," I replied, my voice shaking. "Who are you?"

Before he could answer, the leaf man vanished as quickly as he had appeared. Kaller and I were left standing there, mouths agape.

"Was I dreaming?" I whispered.

We wandered aimlessly, trying to make sense of what had just happened. After what felt like hours, we stumbled upon an opening in the forest. To our astonishment, we found ourselves back in our town, Eveande Carlin. The sky was bright, and the sun was high. It was as if no time had passed at all.

"How... how did we get here?" Kaller asked, his voice filled with disbelief.

"I have no idea," I replied, equally stunned.

We made our way back to our homes, just in time for lunch. The familiar sights and sounds of our town brought a sense of relief, but questions lingered in our minds. What had we seen? How did we get lost and then return so

PINK

quickly? And who was the mysterious leaf man?

As we sat down for lunch, the comforting aroma of freshly baked bread and stew filled the air. Our mothers fussed over us, oblivious to the strange adventure we had just experienced. Kaller and I exchanged glances, silently agreeing to keep our latest escapade a secret for now.

"Pass the bread, please," Kaller said, trying to act normal.

I handed him the bread, still deep in thought. "Do you think we'll ever find out what happened?"

"Maybe," Kaller replied with a small smile. "But one thing's for sure, our adventures are far from over."

With that, we dug into our lunch, the strange events of the day leaving us with more questions than answers. But one thing was

Shanayac

certain: in a world as magical and unpredictable as ours, anything was possible, and our journey was just beginning.

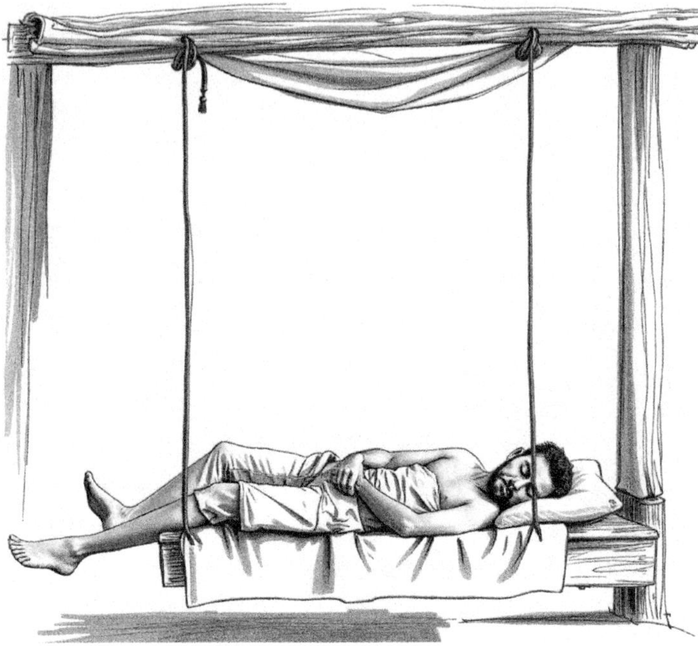

CHAPTER 3

CAN WE TRUST THEM?

Nothing seemed right. In the blink of an eye, day turned to night and back to day again, an impossible phenomenon that now seemed to be our reality.

I met with Kaller, who looked as confused as I felt. "It's as if the planet just stopped. Night hasn't come yet, and it feels like it never will," he said, bewildered.

We wandered through Eveande Carlin, a small but lively town usually brimming with the sounds of daily life. Today, however, a strange stillness hung in the air. One of our neighbors, Mr. Thistleburn, was already asleep on his porch swing, snoring loudly in broad daylight. Kaller and I exchanged uneasy glances.

"How is this happening?" Kaller asked, scratching his head. "It feels like the clocks have gone mad."

Astonished, I checked the clock tower. The large hand pointed straight up at twelve o'clock, but the sun blazed high in the sky, defying the time. We decided to go back to the forest to see if it could offer any answers.

As soon as we stepped into the thick canopy, night fell around us. The moon hung low and full, casting an eerie glow on the mossy ground. We took a few steps back, and daylight enveloped us again. It was disorienting and unsettling.

"Can we trust them?" Kaller muttered, voicing the question that had been gnawing at both of us.

We sat down on a fallen log, unsure of what to do next. Suddenly, a familiar voice broke the silence.

"Hello, Inspector!"

Kaller and I jumped up. "Leaf Dude!" we exclaimed in unison.

The leaf man, now known to us as Bob, stood before us, adjusting his leafy glasses. "And I have a name, you know. It's Bob."

"Bob??" I laughed, Kaller joining in.

Bob looked at us seriously. "No, really, my name is Bob. Is there a problem with that?"

Kaller, looking a bit embarrassed, said, "Oh, he's serious. Sorry."

"Okay, Inspector, what's the problem?" I asked, trying to regain my composure.

Bob sighed. "Something is going on. It hasn't been night for a long time now. People are sleeping during the day, and night just wouldn't come."

"What are you talking about? In the forest, it's completely normal and... wait," I paused,

realizing something. "Don't you notice how quiet the town has become?"

Kaller's eyes widened. "Almost like it's a fake town?"

Bob nodded. "Come with me."

He led us through the forest, stopping at a spot that looked unremarkable. "Go through this door here," he said, gesturing to an invisible entrance.

"Wait, this wasn't here before," I said, stepping closer.

"No worries, I've got you, Inspector," Bob assured us.

We stepped through the door, and suddenly, we were in a small, dimly lit room. The walls were covered in strange symbols, and a single, flickering globe hung from the ceiling. It cast an eerie light around the room, making everything look surreal.

"It's nighttime," Kaller whispered. "And this globe... it's like it's controlling everything."

"What happened?" I asked, turning to Bob. But he was gone.

"Can we trust them?" Kaller repeated, his voice trembling.

We stood there, staring at the globe, our minds racing with questions. The line between day and night, reality and illusion, had blurred beyond recognition. The room felt alive, pulsating with a strange energy.

"What now?" I asked, feeling a shiver run down my spine.

"We need to find Bob," Kaller said resolutely. "He knows something. We have to get to the bottom of this."

With newfound determination, we stepped out of the room and back into the forest. The transition was seamless, as if we had never left. But something had changed. We were no

Sharaya

longer just kids wandering aimlessly; we were investigators in a mysterious case that went beyond our wildest imaginations.

The forest was darker, the trees seemed taller, and the shadows deeper. Every rustle and whisper of the wind sent chills down our spines. Yet, we pressed on, driven by the need to uncover the truth. Bob had vanished, but his cryptic clues and our strange journey had only just begun.

"Let’s go," I said, taking the lead. "We have a mystery to solve."

As we ventured deeper into the unknown, the sense of adventure mingled with fear, making every step an exhilarating mix of excitement and dread. What lay ahead was uncertain, but we knew one thing for sure: we had to find out what was happening to our world and who—or what—was behind it all.

CHAPTER 4

A FLIGHT

Today, Kaller and I embarked on an adventure we had been dreaming about for months. We were going to Nidhy, an airport that would take us to Gogo—a mystical land on the other side of the world where mythical cats and tropical creatures roamed free. Unlike Jojo, our cold and snowy hometown, Gogo promised warmth and wonder.

As we boarded the Riso, the plane that would carry us across the world, excitement buzzed between us. The hum of the engines, the distant chatter of other passengers, and the gentle thrum of anticipation filled the cabin. We settled into our seats, eyes gleaming with excitement.

"You ready for this, Kaller?" I asked, nudging him.

He grinned, his blue eyes sparkling. "Absolutely. I can't wait to see those mythical cats!"

After what felt like an eternity, the plane began its descent. The view from the window was breathtaking. Gogo sprawled below us, a tapestry of vibrant greens and blues. Dense jungles interspersed with crystal-clear rivers and sparkling waterfalls greeted us as we landed.

We disembarked and were immediately enveloped in the warm, humid air. The airport was small but bustling, with people from all walks of life, each on their own adventure. Waiting for us was Loon, our guide—a tall, wiry man with tanned skin and a friendly smile.

"Welcome to Gogo! I'm Loon, and I'll be your guide through the jungle," he said, extending a hand.

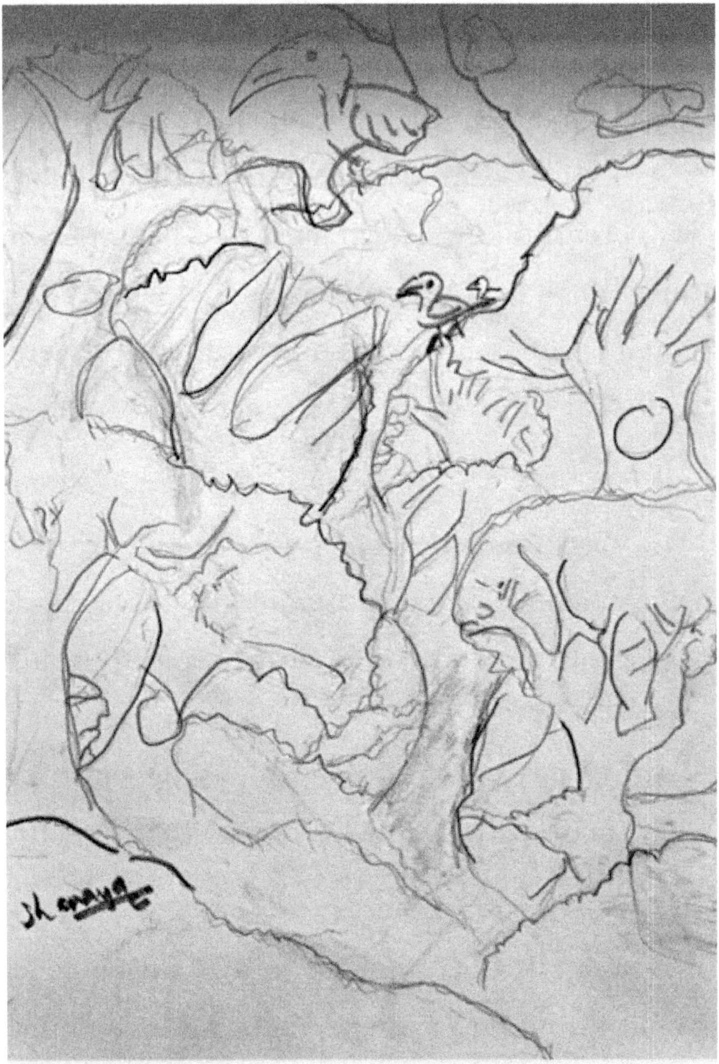

"Nice to meet you, Loon. I'm Dondan, and this is Kaller," I replied, shaking his hand.

Loon handed us safety gear—helmets, harnesses, and sturdy boots. "We'll be exploring some pretty dense jungle, so it's important to stay safe and stick together. Ready?"

We nodded eagerly, and soon we were deep in the heart of the jungle. The lush foliage towered above us, creating a canopy that filtered the sunlight into dappled patches on the forest floor. The air was thick with the sounds of chirping birds and rustling leaves.

For the first few days, we trekked through the jungle, marveling at the vibrant flora and fauna. Loon was an expert climber and navigated the terrain with ease, pointing out rare plants and animals along the way. However, memories of our past encounter with the dragons made us hesitant. Each

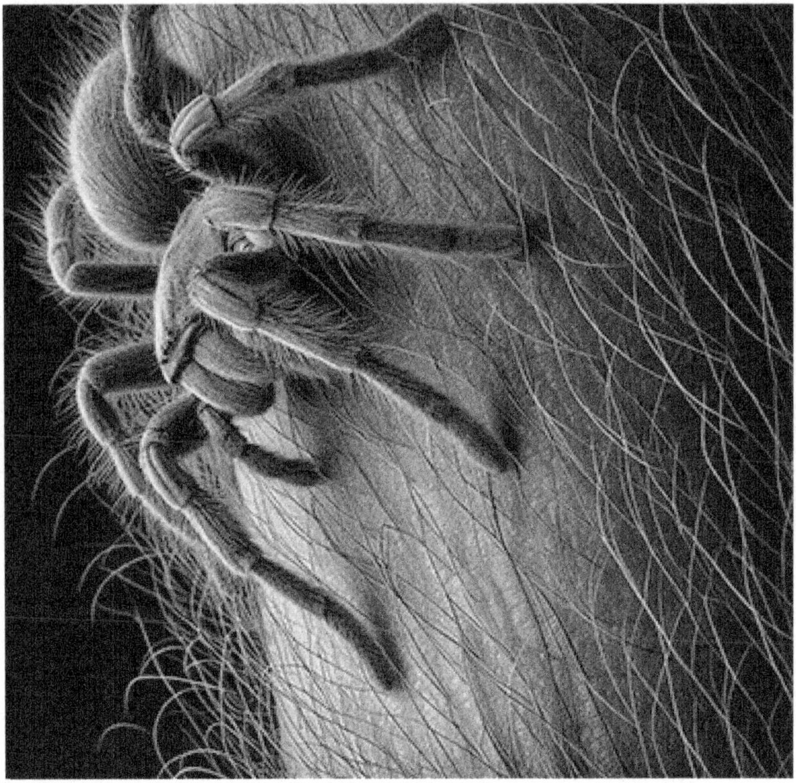

rustle in the underbrush, each shadow, set our hearts racing.

On the fourth day, disaster struck. We were navigating a particularly steep slope when Loon slipped. Time seemed to slow as he tumbled down the rocky incline, his scream echoing through the jungle.

"Loon!" Kaller shouted, but it was too late. Our guide disappeared into the thick foliage below, and a sickening silence followed.

Panic surged through me. "What do we do now?" I stammered, my heart pounding in my chest.

"We have to stay calm," Kaller said, though his voice trembled. "We need to find a way down."

Suddenly, I felt a sharp pain in my hand. Looking down, I saw a miler spider crawling up my arm—a spider known for its deadly venom.

"Kaller, help!" I cried, frozen in fear.

Kaller acted quickly, grabbing my hand and flicking the spider away. "Don't move," he whispered, his face pale. "That was too close."

We were stranded on a mountainside, with no guide, no equipment, and no idea how to get down. Fear gripped us, but we knew we had to find a way.

"Remember that cliff we passed?" Kaller asked, trying to keep his voice steady. "It wasn't too far from the top. If we can make it there, we might have a chance."

Carefully, we made our way to a bumpy section of the mountain that was easier to climb. Each step was a struggle, but we finally reached a small platform just above the cliff. From there, we could slide down to safety.

With hearts pounding and breaths held, we slid down the rocky incline, finally reaching

the cliff. Relief washed over us as we saw a plane flying overhead.

"Wave!" I shouted, frantically waving my arms.

Kaller joined in, and to our immense relief, the plane circled back. A rope ladder was dropped, and we scrambled up, our hearts bursting with gratitude.

As we ascended, leaving the jungle behind, I looked at Kaller. "We made it," I said, breathless.

He grinned, his face smeared with dirt but glowing with relief. "Yeah, we did."

Safely aboard the plane, we were greeted by a team of rescuers. They wrapped us in blankets and offered us water. As we flew back, the adrenaline began to wear off, and exhaustion set in.

"I can't believe it," I murmured, leaning back in my seat. "We survived."

Kaller nodded, his eyes closing. "That was the scariest adventure yet."

Despite the terror and uncertainty, we had come out stronger. And as the plane soared above the clouds, I couldn't help but feel that our adventures were far from over. The world was full of mysteries, and Kaller and I were ready to face them all—together.

Aak

CHAPTER 5

OUR UNLUCKY LIFE

Six days had passed since our harrowing adventure in Gogo. Despite the terror and near-death experiences, we always seemed to survive. Kaller and I couldn't shake the feeling that we were magnets for trouble. No matter the danger, we came out unscathed, yet the questions lingered. Why did we always find ourselves in these predicaments? And why did we always survive?

One morning, the unease gnawed at me. I couldn't stop thinking about our string of bad luck. I was too embarrassed to share my thoughts with Kaller, fearing he would laugh at me. However, as we sat quietly in our favorite bakery, enjoying the warm pastries, Kaller broke the silence.

"Have you noticed how much trouble we get into?" he asked his voice barely a whisper.

I looked at him, surprised but relieved. "I was thinking the same thing but was too embarrassed to tell you," I admitted.

"Yeah, it sounds pretty weird, so even I was scared to bring it up," Kaller replied, his relief evident.

We sat in silence, pondering our strange luck. Finally, an idea sparked in my mind. "Let's go back to the woods," I suggested.

Kaller raised an eyebrow. "Are you sure about that? After everything that's happened?"

I nodded. "I have a feeling we might find some answers there."

Reluctantly, Kaller agreed, and we set off into the woods once more. The dense canopy overhead filtered the sunlight, casting eerie shadows on the forest floor. The air was thick with the scent of pine and earth, and the only

sounds were the rustling leaves and our cautious footsteps.

Midway through our trek, we heard a noise coming from a nearby log. We approached cautiously, our senses heightened by the memory of our previous encounters. To our shock, the log had a face, tears streaming down its wooden cheeks.

"Did that log just...cry?" Kaller whispered, his eyes wide with disbelief.

Before we could react, the log rolled away, disappearing into the underbrush. Suddenly, an alarm blared, and we saw a figure in an orange jumpsuit sprinting towards us, chased by a prison guard.

"Not again," I groaned as the escapee grabbed us by the collars, threatening the guard. We screamed for help, but the guard quickly took out a device from his pocket and aimed it at

the escapee. With a click, the escapee froze, stunned by what looked like a gun.

The guard approached us, panting. "What are you doing out here at this time of night?" he demanded.

We hadn't realized it was night. "We got lost," I stammered.

The guard nodded and began escorting us out of the forest when the log from earlier leaped out of the bushes, shouting, "AAAAAAA!" It tripped the guard and scurried away.

"That bug AH!" Kaller exclaimed, his voice trembling with frustration.

We looked down at the guard, who was lying motionless on the ground. "He looks dead," I whispered, my heart pounding.

CHAPTER 6
THE CHASE

Kaller and I decided to chase after the log, driven by a mix of fear and anger. Kaller picked up the guard's gun, gripping it tightly as we ran. The log stopped in its tracks, glaring at us defiantly.

"Stop right there!" Kaller shouted, aiming the gun at the log.

The log spat on the ground in a gesture of defiance. Kaller, enraged, forgot about the gun and leaped onto the log. The log bucked and twisted like a wild bull, trying to shake him off.

"Kaller, be careful!" I yelled, watching the chaotic struggle.

Eventually, Kaller was thrown off, landing hard on the ground. The log, panting and

visibly agitated, glared at us before disappearing into the forest.

"We need to find that log," Kaller said, his voice determined.

For days, we searched the woods, tracking the mischievous log. Our anger and frustration grew with each passing hour. One night, as we were camping, we heard rustling nearby. There it was—the log, attempting to steal our supplies.

"Not this time," Kaller muttered, grabbing the log with both hands. In a fit of rage, he snapped it in half. The log let out a cry, and for a moment, I almost felt sorry for it.

"That was...intense," I said, sitting down and catching my breath.

Kaller nodded, his face flushed. "I had to do it. That log caused us too much trouble."

As we sat there, surrounded by the quiet of the night, I realized that despite our constant

Sharaya

run-ins with danger, we always found a way to come out on top. Maybe our luck wasn't all bad after all.

CHAPTER 7
THE JOURNEY

As the sun dipped below the horizon, painting the sky in shades of orange and purple, Kaller and I found ourselves deep in the forest. The night was creeping in, and the air was growing colder. Our hearts pounded with anxiety, knowing our mothers were likely worried sick, believing us to be missing. We knew we needed to head home, but the dense forest around us offered no familiar paths.

"We have to find our way back, Kaller," I said, my voice shaky.

"Yeah, but which way?" Kaller replied, his brow furrowed in concern.

We decided to run in every direction, hoping to find something familiar. We sprinted until our legs burned and our lungs felt like they were on fire. But every turn seemed to lead us

deeper into the unknown. The forest seemed to stretch endlessly, with no signs of the town. Panic began to set in, and we freaked out, our breaths coming in short, frantic gasps.

Suddenly, we heard rustling in the bushes nearby. I jumped into Kaller's arms, my heart racing with fear. We stood frozen, waiting for whatever creature might emerge. To our surprise, two younger children burst out from the underbrush, their faces lit with curiosity.

"Who are you? You don’t look like anyone from our town," said the first kid, a girl with wide, inquisitive eyes.

The second girl nodded in agreement. "Yeah, what are you doing here?"

Kaller and I exchanged bewildered glances. "What town?" Kaller asked, his confusion mirroring my own.

"How did you not notice the clearing?" the girl replied, gesturing behind him.

Biswajit

We turned and saw, for the first time, a clearing we hadn't noticed before. It opened up to a breathtaking sight—a city made entirely of grass and stone. The buildings, though natural-looking, were grand and sturdy, blending seamlessly with the surrounding forest.

Before the two girls could leave, Kaller stopped them. "Wait! What are your names?"

The girl smiled. "I'm Shanaya, and this is Amalia."

Shanaya had hazelnut-brown straight hair and matching brown eyes. Amalia, on the other hand, had long, curly brown hair with hints of straightness and striking green eyes.

"We have to go now," Amalia said. "Our moms are calling us to help cook dinner for the town."

"Can we come?" I asked, curiosity piqued.

They nodded, and we followed them to the town. The atmosphere was warm and welcoming, with the scent of various dishes wafting through the air. Townrs bustled around, preparing for the communal meal. It was a stark contrast to our own small town, and I couldn't help but be mesmerized by the sense of community and harmony.

As we wandered around, taking in the sights and sounds, Shanaya and Amalia invited us to join them for dinner. "You can stay with us tonight," Shanaya offered.

The town feast was a joyous event. Long tables were set up, covered in an array of delicious food. Lanterns hung from the trees, casting a soft glow over everything. The townrs were friendly, asking us about our adventures and sharing stories of their own.

After dinner, Shanaya and Amalia offered to help us find our way back home. It was a relief to have guides, as the forest seemed even

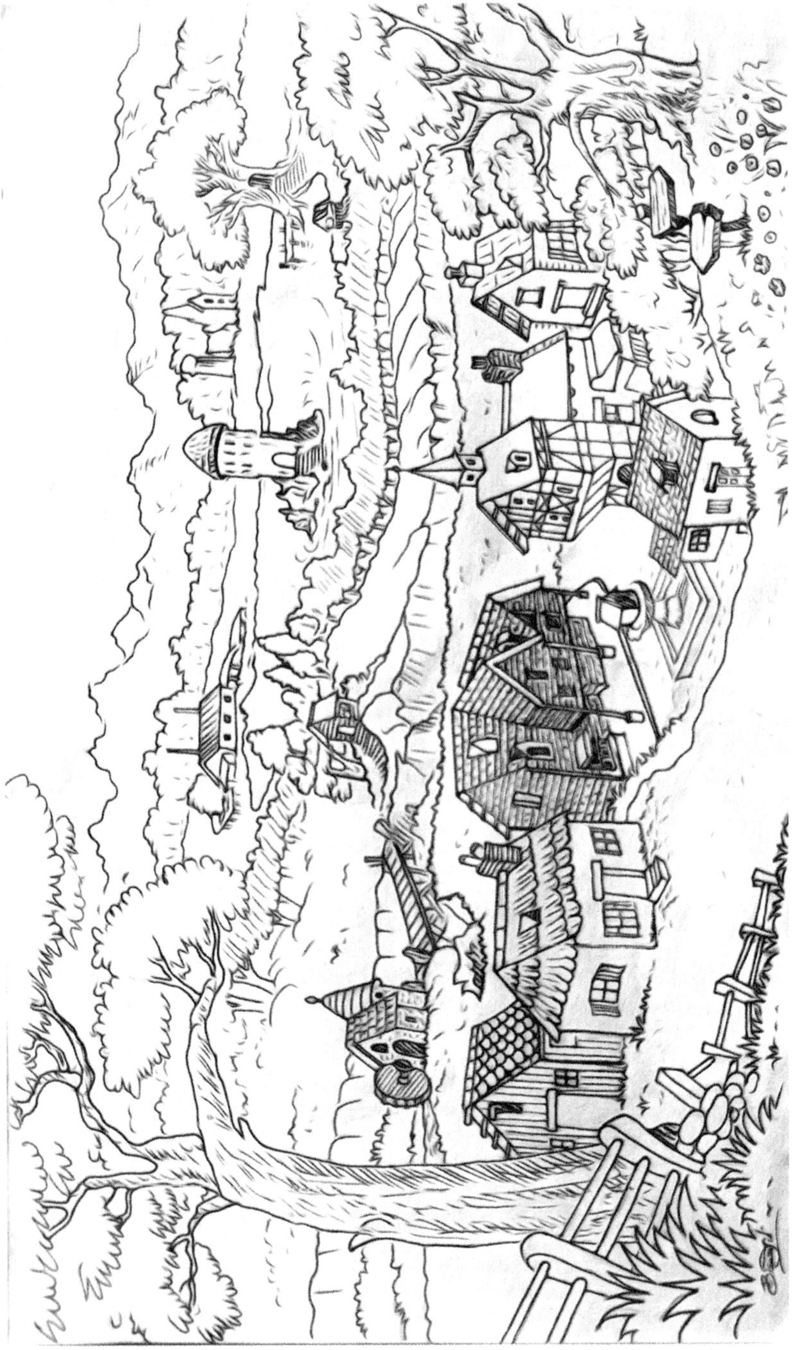

more daunting at night. We made our way through the woods, their familiarity with the paths reassuring us.

When we finally reached our town, we saw missing posters of ourselves plastered everywhere. Our mothers must have been frantic. We headed straight to my house, where my mom screamed with joy and relief upon seeing us. She hugged both Kaller and me tightly, tears streaming down her face.

"Oh, I better tell your mom that you’re back!" she exclaimed, releasing us. A beautiful phoenix perched on her arm, its feathers shimmering in the dim light. "My little friend likes you!" she said, as the phoenix hopped to her shoulder. She handed it a letter, and it flew off into the night.

Minutes later, a different phoenix returned with a letter from Kaller's mom. It danced around us, its magic filling the air with a joyful energy. Despite the fear and

uncertainty of the past few days, seeing our mothers' happiness made everything worth it.

"It's late. You should stay here tonight, Kaller," my mom said, still beaming.

We agreed, too exhausted to argue. That night, Kaller and I had an unplanned sleepover, our hearts finally at peace. As we drifted off to sleep, the events of the past few days played in my mind. It felt like a dream, yet the relief of being home was real.

CHAPTER 8

WE'RE BACK

The next morning, a soft glow from the early sun filtered through the curtains, gently waking us. Kaller and I stretched and yawned, the fatigue from our recent adventures still lingering in our bones. We knew it was time to head to Kaller's house. As we stepped out, the cool morning air invigorated us. Birds chirped merrily, and the scent of dew-covered grass filled our nostrils.

"Ready to face the world?" I asked Kaller, trying to inject some enthusiasm into my voice.

"Yeah, let's do this," Kaller replied, though his voice was still tinged with the weariness of the past few days.

We walked through the town, taking in the familiar sights. The cobblestone paths, lined

with quaint houses, felt comforting. As we neared Kaller's home, we saw his mom standing at the doorway, her eyes wide with a mix of disbelief and overwhelming joy. She rushed towards us, enveloping Kaller in the biggest hug I'd ever seen.

"Oh, Kaller! I was so worried!" she exclaimed, tears streaming down her cheeks. "You're safe. Thank goodness!"

Kaller hugged her back, a rare moment of vulnerability crossing his face. "I'm okay, Mom. Really."

As we entered their cozy home, the warmth and aroma of freshly baked bread greeted us. Kaller's mom fussed over us, making sure we were well-fed and comfortable. It felt good to be surrounded by such care.

Later, we made our way to the playground where our friends were waiting. The playground, with its swings, slides, and

climbing frames, was our usual hangout spot. Today, it felt different, almost like a stage where we would recount our latest adventure.

"Silvia's going to flip when she sees you," I teased Kaller, nudging him.

"Oh great," he muttered, rolling his eyes.

As we approached, Silvia spotted us first. Her face lit up, and she ran towards Kaller, her long blonde hair bouncing with each step.

"Kaller! You're back!" she exclaimed, throwing her arms around him.

Kaller awkwardly patted her back. "Yeah, I'm back, Silvia."

Our other friends gathered around, bombarding us with questions.

"Where were you?" asked Jake, his eyes wide with curiosity.

"Did you see any monsters?" piped up Emma, always the one with a vivid imagination.

Kaller and I exchanged glances. We knew we couldn't tell them everything, but we didn't want to lie either.

"We had quite an adventure," I began, choosing my words carefully. "We got lost in the forest, met some new friends, and... well, let's just say it was a bit scary."

"Scary? Like how?" Jake pressed.

"Let's just say we encountered some unusual things," Kaller added, a hint of a smile playing on his lips.

As our friends continued to ask questions, I couldn't help but feel a strange sense of detachment. It was almost as if everything we had been through was part of some grand story, a feeling that lingered at the back of my mind.

Later that day, Kaller and I found ourselves sitting on a bench, watching the others play.

The playground was alive with laughter and shouts, but my thoughts were elsewhere.

"Do you ever feel like we're in a story?" I asked Kaller, breaking the comfortable silence.

Kaller looked at me, puzzled. "What do you mean?"

"I don't know," I shrugged. "It's like everything that happens to us is part of some weird adventure, like we're characters in a book."

Kaller chuckled. "You read too many books."

"Maybe," I admitted, "but think about it. We've been through so much lately, and it all feels... connected somehow."

Kaller leaned back, contemplating my words. "You know, I've felt that too. Like there's something bigger going on."

We sat in silence for a while, the sounds of the playground fading into the background. I couldn't shake the feeling that our adventures were just beginning, that we were part of something much larger than ourselves.

As the sun began to set, casting long shadows across the playground, Silvia approached us, her usual exuberance subdued.

"Hey, are you guys okay?" she asked, her brow furrowed with concern.

"Yeah, we're fine," Kaller replied, offering a reassuring smile.

Silvia sat down next to us. "You know, we were really worried about you two. It's not the same when you're not around."

"Thanks, Silvia," I said, touched by her words. "We're just... processing everything."

She nodded, understanding. "Well, if you ever want to talk, you know where to find me."

As Silvia rejoined the others, Kaller and I stood up, stretching our legs.

"Ready to head home?" Kaller asked.

"Yeah, let's go," I replied.

We walked back through the town, the evening air cool against our skin. The stars began to twinkle overhead, and for the first time in days, I felt a sense of peace. Whatever lay ahead, we would face it together.

Back at my house, my mom greeted us with a warm smile. "Dinner's almost ready. How was your day?"

"It was good, Mom," I replied, smiling back. "It's good to be home."

As we sat down to eat, the warmth of my family's love enveloped me, pushing away the lingering shadows of our recent adventures. But deep down, I knew that our story was far from over. There were still mysteries to

uncover, challenges to face, and a world of adventure waiting for us.

As I drifted off to sleep that night, I couldn't help but wonder what tomorrow would bring.

CHAPTER 9

DREAM VS REAL

The next day began in a way that was beyond strange—it was downright terrifying. My body felt as though it had been weighed down with lead, making it impossible for me to get out of bed. Every muscle screamed in protest when I tried to move, leaving me completely paralyzed. Panic began to well up inside me, and I weakly called out, "Kaller... Kaller... Silvia... Silvia... help me..."

My voice barely rose above a whisper, and the effort to speak sent a sharp pain through my throat. I tried to look around, but my head felt as if it were glued to the pillow. It was as if invisible chains bound me, holding me captive in my own bed.

"Am I in heaven or hell?" I wondered aloud, my voice sounding distant and unfamiliar.

189

"Why did Kaller and Silvia let me go? Where are they? Are they safe?"

The silence in the room was deafening, broken only by the sound of my own labored breathing. The room around me seemed shrouded in an eerie stillness. The air was heavy, oppressive, pressing down on me with an almost tangible weight. I could see faint, blurry outlines of the familiar objects in my room—the desk, the chair, the bookshelf—but they seemed distant, as though viewed through a thick fog.

Suddenly, the creaking of the door shattered the silence. My heart pounded in my chest as I strained to see who was entering. The door opened slowly, with a drawn-out groan that set my teeth on edge. I heard the soft beeping of a machine and the gentle clinking of metal on wood, as if someone were setting down tools or instruments.

476

“Who’s there?” I wanted to shout, but my voice refused to cooperate. My eyes fluttered, but I couldn’t open them fully. It felt like I was drugged, trapped in a hazy twilight between consciousness and unconsciousness. My mind raced with questions: “What is happening to me? How am I trapped here?”

I tried desperately to move my hands and legs, but they felt numb, disconnected from my body. Fear clawed at my throat, and I cried out weakly, “Kaller… Kaller… where are you? Find me and take me out of this hell…”

The sound of footsteps approached my bedside, each one sending a jolt of fear through me. I felt a sharp prick in my arm, like a needle being inserted. I couldn’t see what was happening, but the sensation was unmistakable. A cold numbness spread from the point of contact, and a wave of drowsiness washed over me.

My mind screamed in protest, but my body betrayed me, sinking deeper into the bed. My thoughts began to blur, and the room around me grew darker. I felt myself slipping away, sinking into an abyss of unconsciousness. The last thing I heard was the steady beeping of the machine, echoing in the darkness.

When I woke again, it was to an unfamiliar ceiling. Fluorescent lights buzzed overhead, casting a harsh, sterile glow. I blinked slowly, my vision adjusting to the brightness. The beeping sound continued, now accompanied by the soft hum of machinery. I realized with a start that I was in a hospital room.

“Where am I?” I thought, my mind still foggy. I tried to move, and this time, my limbs responded sluggishly. I turned my head slowly, taking in the room around me. It was small, clinical, with white walls and a single window that let in a sliver of daylight. Medical

equipment surrounded the bed, their displays blinking and pulsing rhythmically.

"Hello? Is anyone there?" I croaked, my voice raw. The door opened, and a nurse walked in, her expression a mix of relief and concern.

"You're awake," she said gently but with a shock. "How are you feeling?"

"Where am I?" I asked again, my voice still weak.

Memories flooded back—Kaller, the town, the forest. But it all felt like a dream, a series of disjointed images and sensations. "I… I remember being in the forest. I was with my friend, Kaller. Is he okay?"

The nurse nodded without saying a word. She acted as if there was no Kaller.

As I tried to enquire from the nurse, pieces of the puzzle began to fit together, but there were still gaps and unanswered questions. The fear and confusion of the past few days

Shenaya
C4

lingered, but I felt a renewed sense of determination. Whatever had happened, we would face it together. “But, where are they?” I pondered.

The nurse returned with a doctor, and they explained my condition— You were in coma for 2 years.

As the day turned to night, I lay in the hospital bed, my mind racing with thoughts of the strange occurrences, the mysterious town, and the adventures that had led me here. The line between dream and reality had blurred, but one thing was clear: our journey was far from over. My mind was still looking for Kaller and Silvia.

And, I don’t remember when I was out.

CHAPTER 10

A DISTORTED REALITY

I was still groggy from the events of the day as I settled into the hospital bed, the soft hum of machinery and the occasional beeping lulling me into a strange sense of calm despite the exhaustion weighing down my eyelids, a gnawing feeling of unease kept me from fully surrendering to sleep.

As I lay there, a wave of nausea suddenly swept over me, and I sat up abruptly. My head spun, and I pressed a hand to my temple, trying to steady myself. The room around me seemed to waver, as if I were looking at it through rippling water. I took a deep breath and closed my eyes, hoping the sensation would pass.

When I opened my eyes again, I was no longer in the hospital. I found myself in a completely

unfamiliar bedroom. The walls were painted a bright, cheery yellow, and the furniture was simple but cozy. A small desk sat in one corner, cluttered with books and papers, and a window overlooked a neatly kept garden. On the bedspread was a pattern of stars and moons, and a small alarm clock on the nightstand ticked softly.

Confused, I tried to get up, but my legs felt wobbly and unsteady. As I steadied myself, the door to the bedroom opened, and a woman entered. She had warm brown eyes and a kind smile, her hair pulled back in a neat ponytail.

"It's time for school, honey," she said in a gentle voice.

"What's school? And I'm not honey!" I screamed, my voice cracking with panic.

The woman's smile faltered, and she looked at me with a mixture of confusion and concern.

"Why are you screaming?" she asked softly. "What's wrong?"

"Who are you?" I demanded, my heart pounding in my chest.

The woman's face softened with a look of deep sadness. "I'm your mother," she said quietly.

"No, you're not," I insisted, backing away from her. "I don't know you. I don't know this place. Where am I?"

The room seemed to tilt, and I stumbled, grabbing onto the bedpost for support. The woman's eyes filled with tears as she reached out to me. "Please, calm down," she pleaded. "You must be having a bad dream."

Before I could respond, the room began to dissolve around me. The walls shimmered and faded, and the woman's voice became distant, echoing in my ears. I closed my eyes tightly, feeling as though I were being pulled in multiple directions at once.

When I opened my eyes again, I was back in the hospital room, drenched in sweat and breathing heavily. The beeping of the machines seemed louder, and more insistent, and I could hear footsteps approaching rapidly. The door burst open, and a nurse rushed in, followed closely by Kaller.

"Are you okay?" Kaller asked, his face pale with worry. "I heard you shouting."

"Kaller! " I stammered, my voice shaking. "Where were you? I was somewhere else. It felt so real."

The nurse checked the monitors and then my pulse, her brow furrowed with concern. "You had a vivid dream," she said soothingly. "It's not uncommon given your condition and the stress you've been under."

"It wasn't just a dream," I insisted. "It felt like... like I was really there. There was a

woman who said she was my mother, and she talked about school. But it didn't make sense."

Kaller looked at me with a mixture of sympathy and confusion. "Maybe it was just your mind playing tricks on you," he suggested gently. "You've been through a lot."

I shook my head, trying to make sense of it all. "It was too real," I murmured, more to myself than to anyone else.

The nurse gave me a reassuring pat on the shoulder. "Try to rest," she said. "Your body needs time to recover. We'll keep an eye on you."

As she left the room after injecting me; Kaller pulled up a chair beside my bed and sat down. "I'm not going anywhere," he said firmly. "We'll figure this out together." I was almost drowsy

As I closed my eyes, I saw flashes of the yellow bedroom, the woman's kind face, and the

strange sensation of being trapped between two worlds.

By morning, I felt no closer to understanding what had happened.

CHAPTER 11

THE REAL

"Honey, you went to sleep again. I had just woken you up. You will be late."

I opened my eyes and got a jolt. "How am I here again?" I sat up quickly, as if there was no pain in my body, feeling a renewed energy coursing through me. I looked around for Kaller, but he was nowhere to be seen.

"Dondan, I will be late because of you. I have to drop you off today, and you seem to still be tucking your pillow. Get up, bro...Mom has already laid out breakfast."

I turned towards the voice and saw a boy standing in the doorway, his face familiar yet out of place in my mind. "Who are you?" I asked, bewildered.

"Very funny, Dondan. It's me, your brother, Armando. Did you hit your head or something?" He walked over and pulled the covers off me. "Come on, you need to hurry."

I looked at the clock and it was already 8 am. Panic set in as I jumped from the bed and rushed to the washroom, still wondering about my present and the past. My reflection in the mirror looked the same, yet everything felt different. As I splashed water on my face, memories of Kaller and the strange town flooded my mind. Was it all a dream?

After a quick shower, I dressed hurriedly in the school uniform laid out on my chair. The scent of pancakes wafted up from the kitchen, and my stomach grumbled, grounding me in this reality. I ran downstairs, my thoughts still tangled.

"Morning, honey," Mom said, smiling as she set a plate of pancakes on the table. She

looked exactly like the woman from my dream, with the same warm eyes and kind smile.

"Morning, Mom," I replied, sitting down. I glanced around the kitchen, everything looking familiar yet feeling alien. Armando was already wolfing down his breakfast.

"You okay, Dondan?" Mom asked, noticing my hesitation.

"Yeah, just had a weird dream," I said, trying to shake off the lingering confusion. "Where's Dad?"

"Already at work, my boy. You know how busy he is these days," she said, ruffling my hair affectionately.

I nodded, focusing on my pancakes. They tasted like home, and for a moment, I let myself believe that everything was normal. But the nagging feeling that something was off wouldn't leave me.

"Ready?" Armando asked, standing up and grabbing his backpack. "We need to leave now."

"Yeah, let's go," I said, following him out the door.

The walk to school was uneventful, but my mind was racing. The dream, or whatever it was, had felt so real. I needed to talk to Kaller, to make sense of everything. But when we reached the school gates, the familiar faces of my classmates brought me back to reality.

The day passed in a blur of classes and hallways. I kept expecting to see Kaller or someone from the town, but there was no sign of them. By lunchtime, I was feeling more grounded, though the sense of disorientation lingered.

As I was heading to my next class, I felt a tap on my shoulder. I turned around and saw a

girl with curly brown hair and green eyes. "Hey, Dondan? We have Craft together."

"Yeah, I remember Amalia," I said, surprised at how easily the name came to me.

She smiled, a warm and friendly smile that felt oddly reassuring. "You seemed a bit out of it in class. Everything okay?"

"Just a weird morning," I said, shrugging.

"Tell me about it," she said with a laugh. "I've had my share of those. Wanna sit together at lunch?"

"Sure," I agreed, feeling a strange sense of connection with her.

We walked to the cafeteria together, chatting about classes and homework. As we sat down with our trays, I noticed a group of kids from my history class waving at me. One of them was Kaller.

"Kaller?" I called out, my heart skipping a beat.

He looked up and waved back, a puzzled expression on his face. "Hey, Dondan. What's up?"

I walked over to him, my mind spinning. "Do you remember anything about a town? Or an adventure we had?"

He frowned, shaking his head. "What are you talking about? We've never been to a town together."

I felt a sinking feeling in my stomach. "Never mind," I said quickly. "Must have been a dream."

"Okay," he said, giving me a curious look. "See you in class."

I returned to my seat with Amalia, my mind racing. Was it possible that everything had been a dream? But it had felt so real. I needed to figure this out.

That night, as I lay in bed, I tried to piece together the fragments of my memories. The town, Kaller, the strange events—it all seemed like a different life. I closed my eyes, hoping for answers, but sleep came slowly, haunted by the echoes of a reality that might have been.

CHAPTER 12

EPILOGUE

Living with Questions

No matter what, I am still living with many questions. My life has become normal, but I can’t forget the adventurous days I lived in the forest and town. They were so real to me.

As I sit in my room, staring at the familiar posters on the walls and the cluttered desk, I can't shake off the feeling that something profound has happened to me. Was it just a dream? Or was there more to it?

Is it possible to travel to a different world in a dream? This question gnaws at me constantly. I remember every detail of the town and the people in it—their faces, their voices, even the smell of the grass and the stone streets. Dreams aren't supposed to be so vivid, so tangible.

Am I okay? This is a question that lingers in the back of my mind. Sometimes, I catch myself drifting off in class, lost in thought, trying to piece together the fragments of my memories. My friends notice, and they ask if I'm alright. I always tell them I'm fine, but inside, I'm not so sure.

Was I actually in the hospital? Was I in a coma? There was that strange feeling of being unable to move, the beeping of machines, and the sensation of a needle piercing my skin. It all felt so real. But when I woke up, there were no signs of any medical intervention. My parents never mentioned an accident or a hospital stay. Are they hiding something from me?

How could I move from the present to the past and then come back to the present? This question is perhaps the most perplexing of all. It felt like I was living two different lives, each one as real as the other. How can that be possible? Is my mind playing tricks on me, or did I really experience something extraordinary?

Is it my subconscious mind? Maybe it's all in my head, a product of my imagination. But if that's the case, why does it feel so real? Why do I remember conversations, emotions, and even physical sensations so clearly? It's like my subconscious mind created a whole new reality for me to live in.

I still feel something to be missing, something hidden and something unknown. It's like there's a piece of the puzzle that I can't quite grasp. Every night, I lie awake, trying to remember more, to connect the dots. But the harder I try, the more elusive the answers become.

Have you ever experienced this? I wonder if anyone else has gone through something similar. It's a lonely feeling, not knowing if what you experienced was real or just a figment of your imagination. I wish I could talk to someone who understands, who can help me make sense of it all.

Am I still in a dream? This is the most unsettling question of all. Sometimes, I wake up in the middle of the night, drenched in sweat, wondering if I'm still dreaming. What if my entire life is just a series of interconnected dreams, each one leading to the next? How would I ever know what is real and what isn't?

The questions swirl in my mind, making it hard to focus on anything else. I go through the motions of daily life—school, homework, hanging out with friends—but there's always a part of me that's lost in another world, trying to find the answers.

One evening, as I sit by the window, watching the sunset, I decide to keep a journal. Maybe writing down my thoughts and memories will help me make sense of it all. I start with the town, describing every detail I can remember, and then I move on to the forest, the people, and the strange events that unfolded.

As I write, I feel a sense of clarity. Maybe I won't find all the answers, but at least I'll have a record of my experiences. And who knows? Maybe someday, I'll meet someone who has gone through the same thing, and together we can unravel the mystery.

For now, I'll keep living my life, carrying these questions with me. They are a part of who I am now, a reminder of the strange and wondrous journey I've been on. And maybe, just maybe, the answers will reveal themselves in time. Until then, I'll hold on to the memories, both real and unreal, and continue to search for the truth.

Shanayac

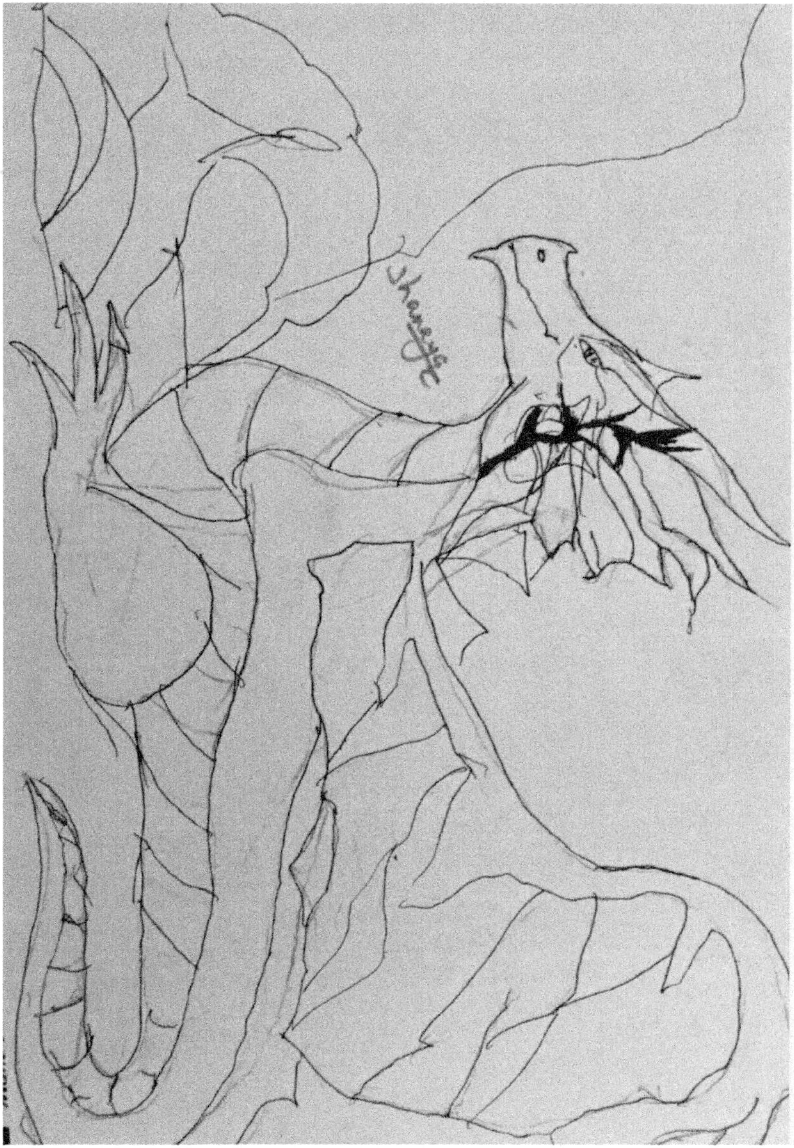

To be Continued...

Printed in Great Britain
by Amazon

47749941R00086